Strangeways

By

Addison Cain

This is a work of fiction. Names, characters,
businesses, places, events and incidents are either
the products of the author's imagination or used in
a fictitious manner. Any resemblance to actual
persons, living or dead, or actual events is purely
coincidental.

Cover art by Simply Defined Art

ISBN: 978-1-950711-32-1

Dedicated to Karen Dee. Thank you for all your help and kindness.

Chapter One

Cliché as it was, I set a cigarette to my lips and struck a match. The quick scent of sulfur, that beautiful moment of burnt wood… then first inhale singed the back of my throat. Nicotine laced smoke swirling through my lungs. Dark air. Dark thoughts. Out of practice, aware that my actions were foolish, the taste of tobacco was no longer one of pleasure as it had been while clubbing in my twenties.

The cheap menthol tasted flat, dirty even.

It tasted exactly how I felt.

The crumpled pack had been going stale in my nightstand drawer for over a year. Couldn't tell you why I'd never chucked it. Maybe I liked the accessibility to a frivolous, expensive pleasure. Maybe I was just lazy in the small spaces where I could afford to be.

I suppose it was providence—there I was, sitting at the end of my sex-mussed bed, sucking on a cancer stick… because.

"Explain to me why your back is to me and a cigarette is in your mouth." Such a soft voice: velvet on the ears—almost a physical sensation to hear.

I exhaled, monotone, and watched the sorry puff of smoke add to the already unpleasant smells lingering in the dingy square of my room. "It's a human post-coitus ritual."

"No, it is not." I heard *him* shift behind me, as if he contemplated edging closer before changing his mind. "It is a formula used in your media to visually style the end of good sex. Should I interpret this act as a sign you were pleased with how I fucked you? I would prefer to be told in other ways that do not cause harm to your body."

Sucking smoke into my mouth, swirling it with a tired tongue, I puffed my cheeks and let it free. A fake inhale. A mutiny.

Which, in its small and stupid way, felt *necessary*.

But he meant well. He must have.

Sometimes it was difficult to tell if the 'new species' were using earthling cues properly. Was he sincere? Did that dusting of hurt in his vocalizations mean anything? Or was he using the manipulations earth men so loved to pepper through their words to garner praise?

How did one even describe sex with these... *men*? "I enjoyed it."

"You don't smoke." The softest rabbit fur, the most lovely of spine tingles. "This is not a habit that is healthy, nor is your current action offering you a sense of joy in this moment."

How the fuck would he know if I smoked or not? Not that it was any of his business...

One last drag. A real, proper inhale. I let burnt air roll around inside me, all the while holding back a building cough. Dropping the cigarette into a cloudy glass of water that had been left for days on my dresser, I exhaled the plume. Watching it shift from strong gray mass into tendrils that twisted into nothing.

3

The darkened air dissipated almost as quickly as my comfort with this situation.

Cutting a shy glance over my shoulder, I forced a pleasant smile. The same one pasted on my face day after grinding day at work. It failed almost as soon as it was born.

One look at him…

Sprawled, utterly naked, propped on an abundance of cheap, mismatched pillows, he waited.

Sure, I was naked too, and he had a great view of the seated top of my plump ass and tapered back, but I was ordinary. Regular.

Normal.

This *man*… lounged, utterly unreserved, blatant in his sexuality. Brazen.

Where some kook had come up with the term 'little green men' to describe his race I'd never understand.

There was nothing little about any of them—not height, not build, not, um, *their parts*—that warranted the diminutive term. The specimen taking up the entirety of my bed was pure muscle, yet lacked the bulk one might imagine came with such strength. There was leanness, definition, in shoulders that were too broad for a human and waist too narrow. Over all that strength was silvery skin, though it did favor green. And just like us humans with our freckles and personal features, there were random defining marks that set him apart from the others of his kind.

Phi had stripes.

Those markings had caught my eye from the first moment I saw him reading a menu at one of my tables. Few and far between, angled to highlight his bone structure, those stripes reminded me more of sexy 1970's David Bowie than any of Earth's exotic animals. The most striking, *my favorite mark*, was a line bisecting his face straight down the center. Down his throat, and now that I'd seen him *au natural*, led to the treasure between his thighs.

"Emily." God, the way he spoke my name was a caress.

He was chiding me for my reticence, for my failure to meet his gaze... and I'd always been a sucker for guilt trips. Up went brown eyes, my attention all his. "Yeah?"

His toes—well, they were similar to toes—brushed my thigh. "Come here. Human women are to be attended to after they have been mated. It is mentally unhealthy for you to draw away."

It wasn't intentional, but I smirked. Phi had a knack for making me do that. "Is that what you've been told?"

Like running water, his tone could be so smooth. Placid, welcoming, *urging*. "We've observed your species for many years."

Shifting onto a hip, I lost my train of thought, a new one smashing in so hard my eyes clenched, my mouth went into a line. I grew tense.

Incredulous, I asked, "You observed humans fucking?"

"How else were we to assure we satisfied? Human females are far more frightening than the males. You must be

6

conditioned to find us enjoyable, or we might be overpowered." As if utilizing a practiced expression, he winked. Hand to God, the alien winked.

And heaven help me, I giggled. I even put a hand over my lips like some sad flirt at a club.

But amusement faded in an odd and unmerciful way. I grew uneasy with the way he stared.

Mouth dry as a smoke-scarred desert, I fought my tongue to say, "You forgot to mention that we find you overwhelming and scary."

Phi blinked his second eyelid, a quick flash of horizontal movement snapping shut over fully black eyes. Like the shutter of an old camera snapping away, those peepers were always active.

Click, click, click, click, click.

There may have been no sound, but when he looked at me, I felt as if he was cataloguing, memorizing every twitch with a mental snapshot. Those upturned eyes seemed a mechanical afterthought of evolution.

Designed to be alluring.

After all, the entirety of him was enticing—the smoothness of his skin, the silvery-green coloring, the slightly oblong skull, even his practically human mouth. But the eyes... they made me feel as if I was a human living on a planet swarming with aliens that should not have been there.

Phi might look mostly human, but shit like that was a quick reminder that these new citizens were not one of us.

Like a languid stroke upon a treasured pet, his voice passed over and through me. "Do not feel fear toward me, Emily."

And with easy words from a lounging tiger, I didn't.

It dissipated just like my last exhale of that disgusting cigarette, fading into calm, steady air.

Still, I spoke of why. "Your kind just showed up here—legions of you—and no one said a thing. Our government, which I will openly admit is populated by warmongering idiots, just stood there, smiling, *waving*, as if they'd sent out invitations to tea. You live in our cities, you even dress like human males now…"

Phi finished my thought, the entirety of his expression gentle. "And the males of your own species are wasting away—have been dying off for generations. The majority cannot survive past forty Earth years and soon will be gone."

Exactly.

And how was it that such a phenomenon was something everyone noticed but nobody talked about? "My brother, he's thirty-eight. He started coughing last year… Tony won't make it to forty."

And while my brother could no longer work to support his family, I was here, having just let an alien fuck me until I'd come so hard I'd torn my cheap covers to shreds.

No longer willing to wait for me to lie beside him, Phi leaned the glory of his upper body forward and reached for me.

Pulled into the cradle of warmth, a defined and powerful chest to my back, I found his touch far more soothing than I should have... considering he was practically a stranger.

His ribs expanded in a great breath, arms closing more firmly around my much smaller frame. He even pressed his forehead to my crown before he said, "Settling on this planet was done peacefully. Not one of your species was harmed. There has been no violence. So, sweet Emily, please tell me the basis of your fears so that I might erase them."

My concerns were so straightforward I could not believe I had to explain. They should have been the concerns of every human. Even thinking of that day their ships blackened the sky, I felt my heart pick up speed. "The atmosphere burned, a wave of massive ships emerging from flame to land where they would. Everyone stood there like lemmings, silent, when you stepped off those creepy things. I saw it on the news, in the streets. *It wasn't normal*."

Exactly! I felt it in my very marrow at that moment those words crossed my lips. It wasn't fucking normal! It wasn't normal, yet we all acted as if it was.

Phi, muscled arms wound around my middle, rubbed his cheek to mine. It was smooth and lovely. It smelled of fresh air and stiff breezes. Of open places outside of city smog.

I took a greater inhale than I had of my cigarette and let it linger just as long in my lungs.

Engulfed by the man breathing at my ear, *cradled*, being treated more sweetly than any living human had ever treated me, my alarm deflated.

I even offered a conciliatory nod when he reasonably explained, "Your film industry has conditioned you to think extraterrestrials only seek out Earth to invade, steal your resources, and commit genocide."

"Not true." His words should not have been amusing, but I smirked as if he'd struck the perfect chord. "The alien species in the original *Star Trek* were all go go-dancing sluts for Kirk."

11

"I enjoy the fact that you are humorous." Phi smoothed his fingers over my sex-tangled curls, tugging playfully to watch a spiral bounce back, and in a way that gave inexplicable pleasure. Then I was enfolded again. Brushing my ear, his lips parted to impart more sweet words. "It was fortuitous that I found you first, Emily."

Chapter Two

Found me? Phi hadn't found me; he'd just walked into a restaurant—like so many people in this dirty, overcrowded, vicious city did. I wasn't memorable, special, or even that pretty. Who had time to be these days?

I was consistently rumpled, past my prime, and doing all I could to work as many hours humanly possible. Yet this guy made it sound as if I'd been discovered in some epic quest.

As if *I* were worth something.

It was disconcertingly laughable. Had I been made of sterner stuff, I might have even brushed it off. Instead, I was horribly embarrassed.

Being embarrassed while naked was no fun. Being embarrassed while naked and held by the man who had just fucked you was even worse.

This was where interludes of this sort tended to curve—an awkward pointing out of my flaws, a bored yawn. Maybe even some light ribbing.

Thick ass, bags under my eyes, blemishes, and corkscrew hair that lacked the definition and bounce expensive shampoos might offer.

Ninety-nine percent of the time, I gave zero shits. But in this instance, I really wished I could crawl deeper into myself and pretend everything was different.

But I was no Cinder Girl.

I hated working in service. I also hated the customers, if I was honest with myself. Something I rarely indulged in. Girls like me didn't live the kinds of lives that allowed healthy introspection—not if they wanted to survive the endless hours, the grueling pace, and the lack of any sort of decent affection.

Girls like me smiled, rolled our shoulders back, and kept our aprons pristine and our cuticles messy.

Girls like me returned to squalor because we were too fucking exhausted to clean up the apartments we lived in.

14

Serving tables was backbreaking work.

It was thankless.

Yet I was grateful to have a job, showed up on time, and smiled no matter who was speaking to me.

Even if I despised them.

Even when I served aliens and humans alike in my section.

At this point, I was not even sure which I preferred.

The new species had been here almost a year, so of course, I'd adjusted to seeing their oversized forms at my tables. They were decent patrons, even. More polite than humans by far.

Phi was not the first I had seen and certainly not the first I had spoken to. He was, however, the first I had fucked.

Which made my belly flip in a strange and unwelcome way.

I was still not sure how we'd ended up at my shitty apartment in the middle of the day.

Had I found a human man waiting outside my place of business for me to leave, I would have pulled out my pepper spray and called the cops. Instead, I'd walked right over to him, pushed my curls behind my ear, and said hello. My voice had even been coy.

Anyone with half a brain knew better.

Phi had embraced the situation with unbridled enthusiasm. Dared reach out his fingers to brush a sweat-stuck stray curl off my forehead. He'd *complimented* me—the softness of my dark skin and hair, the almond shape of my eyes, the beauty of my curves.

Internally recoiling, I outwardly smiled. Trained to please all patrons, confused, tired, desperate.

Had a human man touched me like he had, I would have sent my knee flying straight to his groin. But it had been different when Phi put his hands on my body and told me I should take him home. That I required care and he would provide it.

I'd grown wet right then and there.

16

How fucked up was that?

Calling a car with a simple stretch of his arm, a cab actually pulled to the curb. I could rarely afford one. And in I went, to warmth, to rest for my aching feet, and to my crappy apartment.

I fumbled the key in the lock. He steadied my hand.

I apologized profusely for the mess. Again, he called *me* beautiful.

Me.

Tired, worn-down, me.

The first time he'd screwed me, he'd marched me through my door by the elbow. The piles of dirty uniform aprons littering the floor had been ignored, the pair of us walking over abandoned pizza boxes and fast food wrappers. Once at my lumpy bed, he'd bent me forward, ass up, still clothed.

He'd ordered me to stay just so.

I'd never had a man talk to me like that… or flip up my skirt, pull my panties down, and inspect me. And that's exactly what he'd done. Kneeling, he'd leaned up

17

close, tracing his fingers down the shape of my labia. He'd spread them apart to look deeper, and... I should have been mortified.

It's not like I had expected a tryst. Heck, I was sweaty after the morning shift and wearing an old pair of panties.

It didn't matter. Phi had complimented my scent, shape, and even posture profusely.

And then he had thrust in—right there, just like that. Both of us dressed, my cheek to the mattress. Hell, I still had my shoes on.

And I... I had liked it.

It wasn't until my first orgasm that he'd altered position, undressing us both and laying me back to take me face to face like a lover.

That was the first time I'd seen his perfect, unclothed body... and the part of him he'd put inside me.

Absently, as he'd slipped it back in, I'd wondered if they always started fucking an Earth woman from behind... so we might know how good that *thing* could feel and not scream when it waved our way.

And it had felt good. Better than good.

No one in my past had ever gotten me so worked up. Maybe it was the fact Phi's genitals could change shape. Maybe it was the ring of short, waving, tentacle-like protrusions around it that stimulated clitoris, labia... anus.

Maybe it was that he knew how to fuck.

Earth men were terribly lazy in bed.

He'd thrust in, and noises I'd never before made squeaked out unbidden. Those little fingers around his cock, they teased and stroked, as if he could control each one of them no matter the pace. Two of those tentacles had rolled my clit between their slippery, grasping tips.

Legs trembling uncontrollably, I'd come... gasping.

Phi had slowed his pace to accommodate exactly what would extend the pleasure to my squirmy insides. All the while he'd held my eyes. His expression was hard to read: evaluating, measuring, deliberate.

It, like the pre-sex inspection, should have been unnerving.

The instant it dawned on me that this was strange, that I wanted it to end, he'd started pumping his hips again.

Lowering his head, he'd put his mouth on my dark skin and offered what must have been a kiss to my shoulder.

A *kiss*.

Aliens didn't kiss. All the tabloids made that clear

I thought before he began to pound his hips that what we were doing could be classified as fucking. I was wrong. It grew savage, wild, his feelers grabbing and rough. Inside my body, his cock spread out, undulating up and down its length like a strained soundwave.

Stretching, pleasing, manipulating each nerve.

This was the sensation the most expensive sex toys tried and failed to create. Every last nerve of my pussy was affected. Too much sensation had driven me to beg him to slow down.

My raw-voiced request led to the opposite effect. He'd pounded even harder, rearing back, taking me by the hair to hold my eyes again.

Saturated, endless—the entirety of his eyeballs black in a face that, if human, could have been famous on the silver screen.

These creatures were pretty. They also didn't seem to understand the concept of, "Please, stop."

I wasn't begging out of fear or unwillingness. They were the cries of an overworked nervous system and the fear that the building orgasm might actually cause permanent harm.

He'd only offered four words in return. "You can bear it."

Stuffed full of writhing alien sex organ, pinched and prodded by a series of tentacle things, I'd caught my legs behind the knee and braced against the onslaught. *I'd obeyed.*

And he had practically threatened me in his hissed response. "Good choice."

Good choice? It was the only choice. Spread or be crushed by powerful hips and things that did not go inside nice human girls.

I was so fucking wet.

Rolling snaps of twitching muscle were the only warning that a wild orgasm was about to take hold. My womb clenched, vaginal tunnel wrecked by a foreign invader, and I began to wail.

The noises he inspired in me were anything but pretty. Primal, base, *inhuman…*

Phi dragged me through it until I was a drooling mess. And just like that, he'd stopped. Utterly.

It took long minutes to even consider that he might not have come at all. Maybe his kind didn't do that.

So why proposition me?

No slippery evidence but my own abundant juices waited. He had no testicles, so maybe there was no sperm.

And because I'd lived a life where men came first, I asked, "Did you…?"

He'd settled my panting, sloppy self against his body, tucking my arm around his middle and said, "That was for your pleasure."

Okay…

And that's what had driven me to reach for the stale pack of smokes and the sanctuary of false solitude at the edge of my bed.

Cuddled, the sensation foreign, all I could do was look around, wondering what he must think of this dump. My apartment was poor, cramped, and only had one small window half blocked by an AC unit. Dingy walls I had tried to spruce up with fuchsia curtains to match my bedspread did not alleviate the gloom. My apartment, like my life, was not the kind that attracted handsome men. Or, I should say, handsome men who didn't want to leave right after sex.

Having Phi there was unnerving, and I was not sure what to do with him now that we were done. Feed him? Offer coffee? Ask him to leave?

23

The more I thought about it, the stranger I felt.

Have you ever had that sensation that there was something incredibly terrifying right behind you?

Phi's arms seemed less reassuring, and the more he stroked my body, the more sinister the action appeared. The back and forth of those long fingers, they mirrored my shifting perception of the alien. In that moment, when he was so close, all I wanted to do was weep... no matter how beautiful I found him.

Those ships... so many ships the sky went black.

I'd gone stiff as a board, breathing shallow. I needed him to leave and did my best to persuade such a thing. "Your kind doesn't sleep."

He rocked me a little as if he'd seen the action on television and wanted to try it. "And?"

"I'm getting tired—"

I was released, Phi moving his mass with grace Earth men did not possess. Once standing, he had to stoop

24

fractionally, as my ceilings were low. Bowed, he seemed less threatening. Or was it that he was naked and bore no shame in the display?

And a display it was.

He let me have my unnecessary look. Between his legs, he was not like any human man I'd seen. There was no hair, no scrotum, but there was something akin to a flexed muscle. When it had been inside me, it had adapted, you see, changed its shape, length, and width. That silver green organ had even wriggled and throbbed. Now it hung limp, a shapeless bulge encircled by shortened nubs. His little tentacles had receded, laid flat like unopened flower petals.

And there I was staring at it to the point it was indecent. Rude even.

Feeling the twinge between my legs at remembering what that thing could do, I almost whimpered. I almost begged for more. I could almost feel it inside me again, and whatever terror had been burdening me moments before, flew away on the wings of want.

Swallowing, I forced myself to look up and meet his eyes before I lost the last vestiges of fear.

He spoke. He smiled. "You are very beautiful."

Was I? I looked down at my ruddy hands, at my rug-burned knees, and felt there was no comparison between us.

I had not been born to be beautiful, but to work.

One long finger tracing the pattern of freckles atop my right breast, Phi said, "This I like most. You have stars on you, your own constellations."

Watching him trace out a pattern, I found myself mesmerized.

It was hard to know what he thought, because like I said, I was never sure if he was using human mannerisms in a practiced way to earn a specific response. Therefore, I had to ask, "Did you enjoy…" What was the right word? "…me?"

I could not believe that pathetic question had come out of my dumb mouth.

Immediately embarrassed, my attention went to the scratched wood floor.

He brushed the stiffening tip of my breast. "Very much, Emily. I would eagerly bring you to orgasm again. At this moment, if you desire."

You to orgasm. It was the second time he'd mentioned it was my pleasure and none of his. There had not been *fireworks* for Phi. Sure, he'd seemed focused and involved—as if he found the act pleasurable. But he'd never come... I wasn't even sure if his species ejaculated.

That would be an awkward Google search later.

Out of the blue, it struck me that not once in the last hours I'd lay moaning under this creature had I considered contraception. It was as if the definition of that word had been completely forgotten. In all my adult years, I had never once had sex without a condom. Such an achievement had been something I prided myself on. There were condoms in the drawer by the bed... right fucking there... and I had *not thought of them*.

Long-fingered hands cupped my shoulders, and Phi pushed me gently back to the mattress. "You claimed you were tired. As it is well past the hour you normally rest, I insist you do so now."

Those hands, warm as summer sun, felt good. Eyes growing heavy, I turned into my pillow, imagining the lake. I could feel my skin warm in the sun as I lay on the pier. I could hear the water lapping and smell trees.

I dreamed of swimming with my brother like we did when we were kids. I dreamed of innocence and simple pleasures. And then I dreamed of Phi.

Chapter Three

"Emily!"

That was chef yelling, awful fish-lipped bastard that he was.

In case you weren't sure, I didn't like him. It was hard to respect a man who was usually so drunk he had no fucking clue if he was coming or going. But did the masses laud him for his culinary greatness? *Dare I say greatness with a healthy dose of eye rolling...* Yes, yes the masses did. His food was good; it had put his restaurant on the map in a city teaming with competition, and I made more tips for it.

Didn't change the fact he was a pig.

A stupid, self-absorbed, egomaniacal pig.

It also didn't hurt that he was a man. If you had a dick in my world, everything you did was treated like gold. Speaking of the chef's dick, he'd once told me I should fuck him simply because his cock was hard, and we'd shared a cab home on a cold night. He'd been drunk then too.

He was also married with six kids and consistently smelled of the fryer.

Men might have been in short supply, but gross.

Pushing through the swinging kitchen door, I pretended that my coworkers were not still looking at me as if I'd grown a third eye.

Let's not pretend I didn't know why.

Everyone had been unhappy with me that day. Part of that was my fault. I'd called in sick too many shifts in a row, forcing others to cover for me. Part of it was because, even though no one said a goddamn thing, the staff had seen me leave with Phi almost a week ago.

It had set me apart, simply because it was such an odd thing to do. Alien and human mixed, but didn't, if you get my drift.

It was one thing to have them live with us. It was another thing to let them fondle your breasts on the sidewalk right outside the massive restaurant window.

Not that anyone mentioned the taboo… ever.

You wouldn't find it on the news. There were no alien sex tips in *Cosmo*.

My Google search on alien ejaculation had led to nothing.

So, I did my job quietly and tried to forget; I took a plate of pasta and a burger to table five.

The two aliens ensconced by the window were not seated in my section, which meant I didn't need to talk to them beyond asking if they needed ketchup when I set down their food. Thank the Lord, considering that their kind had made me uneasy since I'd woken up sore between my legs and immediately chickened out of going to work.

Deep down, I felt as if I'd done something very wrong.

I never should have let Phi touch me.

No human male had been allowed such free rein.

And now my livelihood was like a thread over a candle flame; I could feel it in every side eye that stole my direction. Hell, I could even smell it in the air.

Something major had changed.

Looking at the pair at the table, I could not help but wish aliens had never come here.

And then I blinked.

Thinking of it, I assume I wasn't supposed to refer to them as aliens anymore. You see, Phi's kind had matriculated into the system... they were full citizens with the right to vote, to pay taxes... to eat at hipster restaurants.

They even had the right to thank me when I set their food before them.

Turns out, the new kids on the block practiced better manners than their human counterparts. Both smiling, the strangers were gracious.

I turned to go.

"Miss?"

"Yes." I swung around to see if their server had forgotten silverware, or if they needed salt, or maybe their waters were empty. "What can I do for you?"

"Phi would like you to have this."

Oh no.

Don't talk to them. Step backward slowly.

Except my feet took me forward, just as they had done the first time I had seen Phi's lovely stripes.

I still could not tell you what had possessed me to be so brazen. I'd hardly known Phi when I'd invited him back to my apartment; I still hardly knew him... except I now knew what he looked like naked.

And let's make this clear: I was not the impulsive type. I just did my job, chatted with guests, went home with my tips, hung out with friends. Something had been different that day. The shift in formality from waitress and customer to acquaintances... had gone too smoothly in a span of ten minutes.

I'd talked to him. Really talked.

But looking back on it, we'd only talked about me. I could not tell you a thing about Phi beyond the silly fact that a creature named Phi liked to eat pie—blueberry, especially.

I'd snickered about it when I'd brought him his third slice the first day he'd graced my table. Dry humor had always been my favorite

He'd smiled, and God help me, I'd blushed.

As you already know, I'd done more than blush when I found him waiting for me outside that night. I'd been an enthusiastic participant. Having him push inside me felt like the culmination of the perfect date with the perfect guy, not the end of a long shift where I needed a shower and my feet hurt. I was still not sure what I'd said that encouraged him to reach for the buttons of my cardigan or if I'd touched him first.

Had I?

I could not remember.

It didn't matter. All I felt now was used.

Embarrassed.

Stupid.

Guilty.

Alien fucktoy was stamped on my forehead.

The restaurant guest was still waiting, a small box in his extended hand. Blinking out of a daze, I chewed my lip and knew I didn't want whatever was nestled under that shiny white lid. Standing like a statue, I appeared rude, and my natural inclination to be obedient made me self-conscious of just how ungracious I was behaving.

No eyes were on me, but it sure as hell felt like everyone was watching.

The guest remained patient, even under my squinty-eyed scrutiny.

Unlike Phi's silvery green, the markings on the guest's face were purple. They were soft and speckled, almost feminine. And he was dressed in a tailored suit like some sleazy attorney.

Phi had dressed in jeans and a sweater... he'd looked accessible and normal. The alien sitting before me seemed to have weaseled his way into a position of authority. That sentiment of power was even in his voice when he said, "Take the box, Emily."

Next thing I knew, the gift was in my hands. Popping the lid open, I found a cellphone inside. Underneath was a note that read: *Yours must be malfunctioning, as you do not answer when I call. Here is a working replacement.*

I stifled a nervous snigger. Like I'd said, dry humor was my favorite kind.

The modest flip phone in my apron worked just fine, even if it lacked all the bells and whistles of the latest smartphone shining and pretty in that box. I didn't have texting capabilities, not when that extra $15 a month could go somewhere necessary. Besides, what would I need all that for? All I wanted from my phone was a way to call my brother, to talk to his wife and his children.

Everything I needed, I had.

I don't think Phi really expected me to keep the new phone. It was more of a, 'why have you avoided your job for days and ignored me?'

Easy answer. Because I was a coward...

I also really disliked awkward conversations. Sure, I could fake it at work, because none of what I said to customers was real. It was a spiel, a gig, where I just smiled and took orders—story of my life.

Why had Phi even wanted to talk to me after sex? Men didn't do that. Not with girls like me.

I didn't know what possessed me to reach into that box and tap the home button, but before I knew it, the phone's unlock screen flashed to life.

With my audience of two aliens, I stood slack jawed, unsure if I should burst out laughing or be mortified.

Right there, right on that pricey phone's screen was... an alien dick pic.

Chapter Four

Phi's stupid phone sat in my pocket, flattened against my humble flip phone and making a bulge in my apron. Why on earth I still had the thing, I couldn't tell you. I'd just sort of panicked when I should have left it in the box and returned it to the pervy alien's well-dressed chum.

Instead, I'd backed into the kitchen only to be yelled at by my boss.

That, I had deserved. I'd run right into one of my coworkers and knocked a tray from her hands. Food had gone everywhere, broken dishes scattered. Marinara sauce was all over Rosalee's white button-down shirt.

I'd scrambled to clean it up, but... uh... it was pretty clear I was permanently on her shit-list.

And Chef was pissed.

The extinction of our human men—not that anyone would call it that

out loud—had made those who were
thriving an icky type of self-righteous
prick. I found myself unable to like them.
Would they have been so self-serving if
they were not so important to the gene
pool?

Yes, I had deserved to be
reprimanded for my clumsiness, but no
one deserved to be screamed at so loud
even the dining guests could hear.

"Fucking idiot!" Slamming a pot
against the stove, he'd turned, gathered a
bread roll, and thrown it at me. "Get the
fuck out!"

"Sorry, Chef." Dumping a handful
of broken plates in the trash, I demurred.
"Right away, Chef."

Rushing out of the kitchen, hands
sticky with ruined food, hair a mess, and
expression one of worry, I knew at that
moment that I was going to get fired.

The missed shifts, the fraternizing
with guests, the broken plates… it added
up.

Maybe if I slept with Chef like the
other girls did, he'd let me stay.

I sure needed the money.

But, ugh. I knew he'd demand bareback... and I just could not bring myself to do it. The men wanted children, you see. Lots and lots of babies they'd never help raise. Males didn't live long. The population needed to grow. Blah, blah, blah.

My brother was one of the rare birds—a wonderful person, a great dad, and a good husband. He'd never used the fact his lifespan would be reduced to father children with other women outside the bonds of his marriage.

The media called it repopulation withdrawal. Men were encouraged to be prolific, women were encouraged to shoulder the burden of single motherhood without complaint.

And then there was me—the waitress with condoms in her basket at the grocery checkout.

I could not tell you how many dirty looks I have received over the years. Considering that chlamydia and gonorrhea were once again thriving in our society,

I'd take my chances with the occasional disapproving look.

You don't even want to get me started about syphilis or HIV.

No joke, I've had several would-be lovers flat out refuse to fuck me if I insisted they wear one. Those types of exchanges usually ended with the gentleman in question lecturing me on the necessity of our species' propagation. After all, I might be blessed with a boy and uplifted from my crap social standing of childless unwed waitress.

Fuck those guys—and not in the biblical sense.

I was nineteen the first time a boy tried to bully me. Young and stupid, I'd buckled, leading to one of the worst sexual experiences of my life. Nine years later, I no longer let pushy assholes stay in my apartment once they refused to wear a rubber.

As you could probably tell, my sex life was not flourishing.

Childless, almost thirty, with no prospects, I'd settled, even made myself content with my lot in life.

Personally though, I couldn't imagine human men were such jerks three generations ago. Then again, maybe they had always been godawful. I didn't know, and it's distasteful to ask too many questions about the times before. On the upside, it had opened up vast opportunities for women in predominantly male driven career fields. Or I suppose it had—before the new species arrived with their superior technology and eagerness to saturate the workforce.

I was not even sure if I should call them male. I think they are all male... or maybe asexual. I didn't know. They certainly took on male dress and mannerisms. I didn't know if they all had the same thing under their clothes.

Maybe they chose to present as male because it would offer them an edge. For example, there was a rumor that a particularly popular alien sought to run for congress. Men had a better chance of getting elected. I didn't know why that terrified me, but it did. I'll admit I might have even been envious of *his* success.

After all, I'd gotten the short end of the stick. This was it for me.

My father died at thirty-six, leaving my mother with two children to support. My big bro enjoyed an education; I "enjoyed" working at a diner after school to help put him through college.

He was never a dick about it, and if I felt a little bitter, it's not his fault our mother sought to raise him up. That's just the way things were now.

Had I the chance, I think I would have liked to be a teacher. I liked kids, even if I'd been less than enthused about having one with some random guy just because *the gene pool must swell*.

My sister-in-law was a really lucky woman. Or maybe not. After all, she was the one who was going to lose her spouse.

I was going to lose my brother.

Two kids would need financial support, and I'd already been sending them half my earnings every month for years.

Fuck. I'd have to find a new job right away.

"You should leave." Yup, marinara had ruined Rosalee's shirt. There would be no getting that stain out.

If I left now, I'd lose the tips. I needed that money. "I haven't closed out my tables yet."

There wasn't any compassion waiting in the large brown eyes of the waitress I'd pissed off. "Chef wants you out. You're causing a scene standing here staring into space. Just go."

My pocket vibrated, and I jumped, squeaking, "Table twelve is almost done. I can drop the check now."

Rosalee spat, "How am I not making myself clear? You're fired. *Leave.*"

The buzz of one phone vibrating directly next to another annoyed me enough that I grew a backbone and turned on my coworker. "I'll leave when table twelve has paid."

Chapter Five

Feeling pretty sorry for myself, I walked out of the diner with a pocket stuffed with less than fifty bucks.

And a stupid new phone.

I knew Phi's alien buddies had seen and heard what had happened. I was sure they observed me in those final fifteen minutes before I was practically shoved out the door, and I could not help but be angry with the pair of them.

Somehow, this felt like their fault.

No, that was just me shifting blame. It was easier to be mad at strangers than take responsibility for my own clumsiness and poor choices.

There were other restaurants. I'd find another job. Everything would go back exactly the way it always was. I told myself this on the long walk home. The mantra didn't help ease my shitty mood.

Ignoring the constant vibration in my pocket, on the other hand, did make me feel a little better.

I could have silenced it. I could have turned the phone off.

I didn't.

Maybe it made me feel less lonely on that walk of shame. Phi had come to my apartment, had had sex with me, completely for me. He'd gained nothing. Some part of me, the part that was tired of doing everything for everyone else, had liked it more than I should have.

Even with the weird alien dick.

I was almost tempted to answer just to see if I could run away with that sensation again.

I was more tempted to chuck the phone into the street and watch it get pulverized by passing cars.

Instead, I just kept walking.

On my left, smack dab in the middle of my city, was a park where I had played soccer as a kid. There were old trees, a lake, a little segment of wildlife and rugged beauty in the concrete jungle I'd been raised within. People didn't go there anymore.

Now, the park, like so many other places around the globe, was filled with a shining black spacecraft larger than the grandest skyscraper in the glittering financial district.

It annoyed me. And was another thing we just didn't talk about.

Looking at the monolith, at what I knew had been crushed beneath it, I frowned. There had been a swing set not fifty paces from where I stood that I had played on when I was little. I had loved that park.

A nasty glare was all I could offer. And being as it was, I didn't even know if my glare was in the proper direction.

The smoothness of the black ship made it difficult to tell where doors or windows might be located. The glassy surface looked icy, even with the early autumn sun shining so bright I had to squint.

I leaned against the wrought-iron fence and wondered if anyone was inside. Could they see me staring and know how much I disliked that black thing?

Did they sense how I felt?

That ship no one talked about and no one came to see should not have been there. My swing set and beautiful trees should have been there. Aggressive geese and a green lake should have been there!

"Emily." There was almost a question in the way he'd spoken my name. Concern.

How long Phi had been standing behind me, I couldn't say. But I could tell you that deep down I knew he'd be there, invading my sulk over this once great place.

I didn't turn around to acknowledge him, but I did speak. "My brother is dying. He won't survive the year."

I had no idea why I'd said such a thing to Phi, nor did I fully grasp why my voice pointed the blame at him.

Three long fingers reached forward to tousle the mass of my curls, to play with them. I shied, pulling back, my eyes caught in the shutter of his inky pupils.

Click, click, click, click went that silent, unsettling camera.

He still touched me, following my retreat. "The environmental impact your species has had on this planet is catastrophic. The consequences are extreme."

And my species was dying. How many generations could we possibly have left? Maybe that's why they had come here—to wait for us to die off while trying to subvert the pollution before we ruined the earth for them to sweep out from under our rotting feet.

Fumbling in my apron pocket for Phi's phone, I blurted, "I used to play here when I was little. Your ship… it smashed—"

I was cut off when Phi unexpectedly stepped forward and pressed his mouth to mine.

Like the first time he'd done such a thing outside my restaurant, I felt overwhelmed and drunk in seconds. Wrought-iron bars digging into my shoulder blades, I found my body trapped by the fence, the silvery-green male, and a whole heap of feelings I should not have.

And I was really sad for some reason I could not place my finger on.

Trying to mutter things into his mouth was pointless, all it led to was a series of smothered squeaks left to die.

Phi exuded enthusiasm beyond the masterful tongue that was just a little too coarse to feel normal. It was in the way he embraced me, the way he pressed me back as he unhooked the gate beside us.

Drawing me into the park, pulling me straight to that shining black vessel, he had me against it before I even realized what he'd done.

That flawless surface wasn't cold as I'd suspected, but warm from the sun and immensely soothing on muscles aching and tense from a shitty day at work.

Drawing my hand to the bulge between his legs so I might feel it take shape, Phi seemed to promise the very thickness and expanding length were mine, that he'd tailored it to my body and wants.

Graceful fingers undid the buttons of my uniform, parting the white shirt even though we were out in the open. My bra wasn't pretty or expensive. It had no lace or satin. It didn't matter. The cups were tugged down until my nipples popped free, left blatantly exposed. The bent cups shoved my breasts upward so he could pull the tips into his mouth, and I might have moaned in the open air like a whore turning tricks in an alley.

How he knew to knead and pinch, to suck and lick, I couldn't say. His kind didn't have nipples, just like they didn't have belly buttons, but every time he toyed with mine, it sent a shot right between my legs. Head thrown back, my weight supported by the angle of the ship, I clung to the thing that distracted me from all my concerns. When he broke the button on my slacks and yanked them down, I let him free one leg completely and hitch me higher to wrap my limbs around him without the burden of cloth between us. His fly was down, my legs were spread, and with one sure thrust… that instrument with its frenzied ring of writhing tentacles was fully inside me.

Anyone on 11th Avenue could see, not that I had the mental capacity to register the aliens who'd paused in their journey to observe from the street corner, or wonder about the various occupants' views from houses far nicer than my own. Panting as if I'd run a marathon, I ground against each maddening lunge, breathing his name, begging.

Overwhelming need to be so full of him—nothing else mattered—obliterated everything else in my head. In that moment, I'd forgotten my rotten morning, my anxieties, my brother, the crushed swing set under the ship… *my name*.

I would have kneeled at his feet.

I would have taken that pulsating cock in my mouth and let it wriggle down my throat for the world to watch.

I was drowning, and he was clean air, his organ shifting to scratch at my every last nerve until I was twitching and making noise no dignified woman would ever moan even in the most twisted private moments. I felt him throbbing in time with my heart, wondered if he'd curve his cock the way he had the last time we'd fucked, until that sweet spot was tickled, and I felt like my clit might explode.

He did, and I screamed.

The swell between my legs, the way he pulled at my pussy lips and undulated until I might burst, would be my death. Phi rode it out. He dragged me through it and filled all the places inside where I'd always felt empty.

I felt *alive*.

And then it was over.

The aftershocks of my orgasm were almost painful, and I knew my face was scrunched up, that my mouth gaped open, and that I had gushed an obscene amount of fluid to dampen the alien's open trousers.

He was so still, watching me fixedly, those pupils changing though his eyes never moved.

Pinned against the ship, my legs around his middle, I felt his grip on my hip tighten as he mashed his pelvis forward as if to punctuate what we had just done.

And then I felt more…

There was a change in that organ. A manic fluttering as if what had been smooth had sprung—I didn't know how to explain it—*feelers*?

Squirmy, I tried to find the strength to tell him I was finished with that ride.

"Be still." His voice, it was heavy with command and thick with *his pleasure*.

It was too much. Too much feeling and fullness building up inside me, to the point I could even see movement ever so slightly behind the flat of my stomach. Those searching things invaded, and I began to cramp when they all seemed to find what they were looking for and dove in.

He had not done this the time before, and I found I wanted it to stop. His second hand flew to cover my mouth when I started to protest. He fused us, his face one of ecstasy when the tiniest of slithering things breached my cervix and entered my womb.

The feeling was like the poke of a Pap smear swab, uncomfortable and sharp.

Moments later, I jumped when I heard a loud pop. It was him, and whatever had caused the sound had given him a fantastic release. He groaned in a way that made me feel utterly filthy. But that was the end to it. Those horrible things retracted, my painful cramping ended, and his deathlike grip on my body grew gentle. Sweet.

Phi's lips went to my neck, the man pressing kisses to the flesh. "As my body continues to adapt to yours, the discomfort will recede. Soon, you will enjoy it."

What the fuck had he just done to me? My hands went to cover my swollen breasts, my eyes darting between our bodies to confirm that it was a smear of blood I saw on his cock. I wasn't sure if it was mine... or his. Did they bleed red?

I began to shove.

The way he took my jaw and made me meet his eyes, I felt like he was speaking to me. Saying *I did not do this the first time we fucked because I needed*

you to know how much pleasure I might
offer. It won't always hurt. All is well. This
is what I am. This is what you are.

Then he kissed me, and it was soft
and promising, the brush of his mouth
careful.

The ship no longer felt warm on
my back. The sun had gone, the two of us
having humped like stray dogs for God
only knew how long. The second I
shivered, he warmed his hands up and
down my arms. He called me pretty.

And I, I felt as if I'd been tricked.

Chapter Six

Holding hands with a creature that had only three extremely long fingers wasn't as awkward as you might imagine. Trying to keep busted pants from falling down during said walk was. My apron hid the damage to my trousers, but either I'd lost weight or the darn things were torn worse than I thought—with every step, they had to be hiked up.

It was far more distracting than the feel of warm alien skin against my palm.

"Have you eaten today?"

"Yeah," I lied, trying to hook my thumb under my belt loop to pin my damn trousers in place. "I ate at work."

He paused our parade, my walk of shame. "Why not tell me the truth?"

Because now that I was unemployed, I didn't have any money for food. Missing a meal or two wouldn't kill me.

And it was none of Phi's business.

More important, my thoughts on the matter were not spoken aloud, because I was glaring at him, my feet refusing to budge another step. "Reading my mind?"

A soft smile came to his mouth. "When you lie, you squint."

"Can you read minds?" It was rude, the way I accused in that one question. But at that moment it seemed a very valid question.

He did not react to my suspicions, my subtle hostility, or my attempt to unlace our fingers. He held on and spoke plainly. "I can read your every expression, the cadence of your heart, the way you smell, your tone."

I had a very unsettling feeling there was so much more to it. The heart he'd just mentioned began to race, my breath grew shallow, and I muttered, "That does not make me feel very safe."

"It should. Just think of how well I'll be able to take care of you."

"I can take care of myself."

"I have seen your living conditions. They are subpar, cramped, and

58

dirty. I will do a better job providing what you need."

It was almost funny how simply he spoke of managing my life... as if he had a right to do it. "I'm not a pet, Phi. You can't just take me off the street and keep me."

He turned his black shutter eyes full upon me and said, "But you want to come to my home, don't you? You want to know more about me?"

The markings on his face were darker than I remembered, distracting. Even his jaw seemed more masculine, more human. Had he always had full lips?

Suddenly cloudy, my attention was totally lost on where we were or what we'd been talking about. "What?"

He smiled at me, stroked his fingers across my cheek. "You claimed you were hungry. I was asking where you'd like to eat."

I did have a favorite food. "Have you ever had Chinese food? There's a great place near my apartment." Mentioning my apartment drew my brows low. There was something about it; something that I'd forgotten. "I think I left my keys at work."

Going back in there with my clothes mussed and my pants hanging down was not an option.

I'd never live it down.

"Emily, why don't you stay the night with me? We can order Chinese food from anywhere you desire." Fingertips trailing along my neck, Phi added, "Don't you want to get to know me better?"

I didn't even know what he did for a living. Considering I'd had sex with him twice, that I was holding his hand in public, it did seem a bit neglectful on my part. "I don't know…"

"You will be perfectly safe with me."

The dampness in my underwear distracted me. It was slimy, and I had a feeling that had my pants not been black that they would have had a small red stain. And *that* seemed incredibly important to point out. "It hurt."

Soft and commanding, he reminded me, "But it doesn't hurt anymore."

Exhausted, I yawned despite the poor timing and shook my head. Aliens didn't sleep. He would not have a bed, or fluffy pillows, or warm blankets. "I need to go home. We'll save the date for another time."

"But you don't have your keys, remember?"

* * *

I had to be dreaming.

So comfortable I almost fought my body's mandatory wake-up stretch, my eyes observed a view over the city that definitely did not come from my apartment window. *My* window overlooked a brick building about three feet away. This window displayed the majesty of downtown. I could even see a blue sky.

My sheets were not this soft; my second-hand mattress was not this comfortable. I wasn't even waking up hungry.

Because I'd had a big dinner and grown so sleepy that powerful arms had carried me from a polished table as black and shiny as an alien ship and put me down in paradise.

A strong hand squeezed my hip, the feeling of a lithe body at my back moving in unison with my stretching. "Did you dream?"

I always dreamed. I was still dreaming because I didn't feel awake at all. So what did it matter if I confessed? "The lake…"

"What were we doing at the lake?"

I smiled, turning into arms that were open to hold me. "Laughing in the sun."

Snuggled to a broad chest, I blinked. Silvery-green stripes too beautiful to describe were glimmering before my eyes.

My brain snapped to attention.

This was Phi's apartment, his bed. Why did he even have a bed? Pressing back to take in my surroundings, I sat up. Surrounded in a down duvet, more pillows at my back than even I possessed in my sad attempts to make my apartment hospitable, I was cocooned but utterly naked.

What the fuck?

A strong arm followed, settling around my waist while my host looked up at me.

It was too weird for words. "Are you cuddling with me?"

"I am."

"Why?"

"I wanted to."

Why waste the time? "But you don't sleep."

And now that I was awake, I knew it hadn't been him in my dream; it had been my brother who'd been laughing with me at the lake. It had to be. I'd never once heard Phi laugh. His species might not even be able to produce such a sound.

"Why are you concerned with what I do and do not do? Why not imagine that I remained at your side because I enjoy being near you. It gave me pleasure. It gave you deep, relaxing slumber. Does no one in your life ever do anything for you just because they want to?"

What did that matter? "No."

"So you consider your neglect customary?" He nuzzled his nose to mine. "I'll change that."

"I'm not neglected." There was no one in my life, so no one could neglect me.

"When I offer you things it makes you nervous. When I give you pleasure you grow wary. Yes, you are archetypal for the neglected human."

Growing insulted, I thinned my lips. "And what are you?"

"Smitten with a pretty, neglected human." Quick and smooth, he leaned up only to push me back against the pillows and hover over me. He even looked smug.

It was a strange expression on an appealing alien face. A face I swear to you was different than it had been the first day we'd met.

"While you slept, I considered what is to be done. How would I convince you to enjoy this room I decorated for you? What negotiations must be offered to get you to eat the foods gathered and waiting in my fridge? Would you fight such a beneficial arrangement on the grounds of female independence? You do seem to enjoy being belligerent."

Belligerent? "Excuse me."

He kissed me, lips lingering on my forehead. "Yesterday, you called yourself a pet. Do you see yourself as unworthy of positive attention? Maybe I do want to keep you. Maybe you'll have no choice in the matter."

He was teasing, I could tell—as if he'd just learned the nuance of this type of human interaction and could not wait to apply it. "Phi, I need to go to the bathroom."

"Can it wait?" He took a handful of my breast and began to knead it while simultaneously toying with my nipple. "You were so tired last night and needed rest. Now that you have slept, you need something else."

Breath leaving my body on a sigh, I leaned my head back against the pillows and closed my eyes. He took it as an invitation to add his mouth to the mix.

Taking his time, he learned the ins and outs of my breasts—what made me gasp, the exact kind of friction that increased my arousal.

He stroked and kneaded and *learned me.*

My thighs were already parting of their own accord, but my mind was caught on one final thought. "What do you get out of this?"

His form shifting lower, his mouth grazing my belly, he muttered, "You," before dipping lower.

The modern male did not generally perform this act. They got straight to business or demanded it be done to them. Sure, I'd sucked a few cocks over the years, but no one had ever kissed me *there* before, and my toes were curling before I could stop myself.

God, it felt amazing. Little licks of an abrasive tongue, the sweet sweep of a finger over a slippery entrance. When Phi sucked my clit between his lips, when he speared me with that long digit, I arched off the bed and made a grab for him.

Gibberish. I knew I was speaking gibberish.

My hand to his smooth skull, I watched him devour me. Those alien eyes followed all I did, watched me writhe and yowl. It was too much.

Coming hard, I ground against that torturous mouth, grunting like a rooting pig.

And it was glorious!

No one in all my life had ever made me feel so good.

Glued to the bed, to echoes of pleasure, I failed to move as he crept forward, his alien cock already in the shape he intended to use on me. I didn't, couldn't resist.

Pliant, I let him slip that flapping organ inside. I even peeked down to find the little tentacles manipulating my labia and clit. Bracing his arms so his body remained elevated, Phi made it so I might watch.

The whole thing in my view, familiar now with what that beastly organ could do inside me, I grew excited to an embarrassing degree. Sometimes he would swell within me. Moments later that organ would curve, undulate, or wriggle. It was never like the ordinary tubular shape of a human dick.

Human dick would never compare, and that thought struck me as equally exciting and awful. Nothing would ever be better than this. I'd been ruined for my own species.

As he pumped, as he used me, I think I even began to weep.

Orgasm twisted up, coiled along my spine, brain little more than a mush of feeling. Nails to his back, I left a mark. It was only fair; he was marking me even if the tattoo was invisible. It would never wash off. It would never heal.

My aggression drew out his pleasure. Even while my pussy still clenched and spasmed, he unleashed those things that would bring pain.

Like he'd promised the day before, I found that despite the cramp, I *liked* it. Invasion. Needle-like barbs slithered through me deeper than before.

Into places of my body where foreign objects could cause great harm.

This was how I was going to die.

Pop.

The man cried out, low, guttural, and *alien*.

Pain retreated. Life bloomed where darkness had crept in only moments prior.

I lived.

My pussy clenched down as if to keep his wriggling tentacle of discomfort inside my core.

Traitor vagina.

We were both panting when it was done, each staring at the other. Each mesmerized.

I didn't wince until he began a careful retreat, and it was then I registered how much it actually hurt.

I'd been skewered. Truly penetrated.

There was blood I didn't need to glance down to register.

Whimpering, I lay still as if that might save me. I even pled with my tormentor. "What did you do to me?"

A male who could not look more pleased. Maybe he even looked deeply in love. "You're glorious, Emily. Absolutely perfect."

I wanted to press my hand between my legs and curl up. I wanted to cry. But his massive body still rested in the trembling cradle of my aching thighs, an unmoving monolith.

Cooing over my breakdown, he insisted, he nuzzled. "Be still and let it happen."

But he was done, right? What was to happen? Why be still?

I really was going to die. Is that why these invaders had come? Was I to be dinner? How had I ended up in this room?

"Shhhhhhh." One large hand began to rub my swollen belly. The little bump of flesh that protruded where it never had before. "There is no need to be frightened."

I asked again, faint, and suddenly too tired to keep my eyes open, "What did you do?"

"I gave you a gift."

Chapter Seven

Waking with a start, I sat up, hair a mess. And I really did need to pee. Phi was not in the room to stop me from darting out of bed. He wasn't there to pin me down, or eat my pussy, or fuck me with his fucked up tentacles that tore a person apart. This was my chance.

After I made sure I didn't piss myself trying to get home.

The en-suite bathroom was very fancy, but I was too distracted with a need to urinate and escape to take much notice of it.

I used the toilet, rushing to the sink afterward to wash my hands.

And screamed.

There was a woman in the mirror staring back at me. A woman I had never seen before.

Her hair was longer than mine by a good six inches, and her skin was clear, not a blemish, no dark marks under the eyes or a single wrinkle. She was radiant.

And she dared to look like *me*.

Phi busted through the door.

Unsure what to be more upset about, I looked from mirror to male, back and forth, coming unglued. Because what the actual fuck was going on?

As if he realized his display of emotion only fed into mine, he went calm as placid waters. "Did you dream?"

"What?" What the fuck kind of question was that? "What the hell is going on?"

"You are upset." A statement for the ages.

So much more than being upset led me to grab the nearest thing—an unopened toothbrush packet—as a weapon. I didn't know where to begin. I was naked, in a strange place, *with a very strange creature*. Dried blood still crusted the soft skin between my thighs. And I needed to get out. "Where are my clothes?"

"I destroyed them. You will not require them here. The temperature will be maintained for your comfort."

My phone, wallet, and keys had been in my apron…

Eyes going wide, I knew—knew down to the bone—that my keys had indeed been in the front pocket. Why had I thought otherwise?

"You are messing with my head. It's what you green men do!" Screaming, panicked beyond measure, I threw the unopened toothbrush at him. "You invaded our world! You tricked me into coming here!"

Click, click, click went those black eyes. "It is unhealthy to allow your blood pressure to spike in this manner. Please, take a breath and calm yourself."

Sucking in air, I tried to hold it even though my chest was already forcing it out. I took a breath. I took another.

"Sit here."

My legs wobbled, muscles tensing in rejection of the movement even as I stepped to the toilet and sat down on the lid.

Swiping a glass from the sink, Phi filled it with water then held it out to me. "Drink."

I didn't want to, I really didn't want to. But cool water found my lips, and before I knew it, I'd swallowed the whole thing.

Yet tears were running down my cheeks. Ugly crying, snot and all, I asked, "Why are you doing this?"

Silvery green arms bulging with muscle and power and more strength than any earth male possessed, Phi crossed his arms over his chest. As if he posed. As if to show his feathers, the proud male peacock seeking to attract his mate. "Because you are upset and I do not wish for you to cause harm to yourself."

The only harm I wanted to cause was to the man who'd done things that left blood on my thighs.

Finger to my now flat belly, I felt every bit the living bruise. And let my glare fall upon him with the weight of every last bit of shit I had permitted for all males of all species all my goddamn life.

Phi gave me my glare.

He gave me patience.

Kindness.

A three fingered hand took the glass when I crumpled forward. Head between my knees like a rag doll, limp and aching and utterly a mess, I curled up. Eyes on the marble tile under my toes, tears fell.

Phi ran strokes down my spine as they did. The bastard dared coo over me.

"I'm not a cat!" Though I hissed just like one.

His large hand did not waver in its caress. Voice bearing no anger at my outburst, he commanded, "Stop with that line of thought. My kind does not consider you pets, though we do intend to keep select females in a manner that you might equate with one. Adjustments will have to be made on both sides for assimilation to function optimally. Hear me, Emily. You will be happy like you were in your dreams of the lake. Remember?"

Why trick me into coming into his apartment? Why seduce? He could have just grabbed me on the street and taken me that first day, and we both knew no soul would have looked for me.

Except my brother and his wife when the monthly deposit did not go through.

Jesus.

Muttering against my knees, I grew as fierce as a trembling, terrified woman might. "I want something to wear."

"Anything you desire I will provide." And he proved it by stripping off his button-down shirt, wrapping it around my body with reverence.

Chapter Eight

It was awkward sitting on a barstool with no panties. The button-down covering my breasts was not long enough to offer any real barrier between my ass and the buttery leather. I was sticking to it thanks to what still leaked out of me—just as Phi was sticking by my side.

A bowl of fresh strawberries, cut up for easy eating, were bright as rubies in a bowl. A treat I'd not indulged in for some time. Such a temptation that I forgot the red smearing the seat and took a taste of forbidden fruit. It felt like years since I'd tasted something so fresh.

Fast food was much more affordable than unblemished produce.

I mean, it's not like I never ate a salad, but real fruit… this was a luxury I could not afford.

Gorging like a maniac, I hardly chewed. The berries tasted too good.

Sunshine and earthiness, nature and health, things you didn't find in the city.

Flavors my body craved.

"Has this made you happy?"

"Mmmhh." That's all he was getting from me. A grunt and a quick swallow of cool water, and I was right back digging into the bowl.

He'd wanted me to eat the provisions he'd gathered for me in his fridge. I was not about to turn down free food. But, still unsure what that meant, I'd sat where he'd pointed and glared while he'd prepared the fruit and served me.

That's right. Once he'd convinced me to leave the bathroom and limp out to his gorgeous, shiny kitchen. He'd served me, the waitress.

The irony was not lost.

I wouldn't even have to leave a tip.

Mouth full, ungrateful as could be, I demanded, "I want my clothes back."

Alien shoulders shrugged. "They're gone. I did not anticipate this reaction or I would have asked you first, but understand, Emily, they were torn, stained, and ruined. New clothing can be procured if it means so much to you. But, wouldn't you rather feel the sun on your skin?" He paused, looked me over, and added, "It's such beautiful skin."

Beautiful, my ass. That woman in the mirror was a hallucination brought on my too much overly rough sex. "Where is my phone?"

Phi watched me, noted that I was no longer shoveling food between my berry-stained lips, and formulated. "Who do you wish to call?"

"You can't keep me in here…"

"Why would you not want to stay?" It was as if the alien was actually confused by my irritation. "There is food, comfort, safety. Tell me what you need to be happy in my company."

Angry. Maybe even angrier than I should have been considering my time in his home had been pleasant with the cuddling and the orgasms and the strawberries. That's right, he *had* offered food, comfort, and safety. And like a snuffed out candle, so went my temper. But not my purpose. "I want my phone, my wallet, and my keys."

He opened a nearby drawer and pulled my personal effects out to set before me on the counter. And then he said nothing. Waiting.

Tentative, my fingers reached out to brush the scratched casing of my flip phone, to test that it was really there. Solid plastic met my hands. I opened it to find the battery dead. The jagged coolness of my apartment keys were palmed next.

Dragging my eyes from my things, I looked at Phi. Massive as he was, he looked so utterly crestfallen. And I refused to fall for it. "Why didn't I think I had these last night?"

Large, imposing, but standing in a way that hinted at timid, he confessed, "Emily, I enjoy your company. Is it so hard to imagine you might enjoy mine as well? That subconsciously you created an excuse to be rescued after your terrible day?"

How could I answer that? There was way too much stirring about in my brain to even fathom what to say. "Rescued from what?"

"The same emotion I feel. Loneliness, lovely one." Leaning his mass forward, he rested his forearms on the gleaming counter and stared directly in my eyes. "Having you nearby is like a breath of fresh air. Please stay and let me learn how to see to your comfort. I am willing to put in a great deal of effort."

Why? Who cares about a dumb waitress who didn't matter at all? "Do others of your kind engage in this... behavior? Do they *pursue* other girls? Other... humans?"

Closer he leaned, Phi *click, click, clicking* his eyes. "They do if they find a woman that interests them. It's no different than your concept of courtship. It's a beneficial arrangement for both parties."

His enthusiasm seemed peculiar, so I pressed. "So human females are a passing amusement? A taste of local flavor?"

Running his thumb over my pouty lips, Phi offered his opinion. "Everything about you has caught my attention. I have never desired someone to the point I entered an *amorous* state. We are a monogamous species. You are the only female I will penetrate and assimilate. This is forever."

Forever should have been the ticket that sent me running out the door. But no. Another word sent eerie tingles up my spine. Every *Twilight Zone* episode, every sci-fi film, all of them held this underlying theme. "Assimilate?"

Gracing me with a smile that would have melted any stone-cold heart— if he'd been human—Phi purred, "Our pairing is more natural than the water in your glass or the division of a cell. You've noticed already a tangible adjustment between us. I take on the traits you require, and I enhance you in return."

He was being so direct and smiling so sweetly that I felt my spiking panic to be *wrong* somehow. I even took another sip of water before I calmly stated, "I didn't give you permission to change me."

He nodded, as if to disagree. "Four times now you've accepted me completely into your body. Twice I've both given and taken just enough to assure progress between us." The flat black of his eyes changed, smoldered if you will, and I felt as if he was considering pulling me up to the counter and giving me a stern talking to. "My position in your life, your placement in mine, is inevitable."

Phi had never been firm with me. It was always suggestions he'd employed, even a sense of shyness I'd found appealing. Sitting there, his form towering over mine even though he leaned over the counter made me feel... demure, intrigued, angry, even a little turned on.

The alien was definitely interested in seduction. In fact, though the counter was between us, I was certain his organ was beginning to form into a tempting shape. In my mind's eye I was already imagining him taking me bent over the granite, the cold shocking my stiff nipples to the point I'd gasp. "You manipulate me. I know you do."

"You are incredibly perceptive for your species. That aptitude has drawn the attention of many of my kind. Though I was fortunate to discover your rare trait first, the truth is, if it hadn't been I who staked a claim, it would have been another. My brethren do not all practice the same technique. I have chosen to be gentle in rearing my life partner. I have only offered suggestions. I never *made* you do anything. Others would have used force, hidden you away until transition was complete or you were pregnant and dependent."

Blood running cold, I couldn't help but recognize that I had been somewhat dragged away, stripped of my clothing, and trapped. "Are you threatening me?"

"I'm warning you that aggressive others have already taken notice. We are a competitive species when it comes to seeking mates. I have removed *several* challengers already, made a public showing of my claim, but nothing can be assured if you are out of my sight. There is a natural attraction between us. You may not feel the same attachment to the next of my kind to penetrate your body in an attempt to assimilate a life partner."

Horror sat plain on my face. "Are you telling me that right now women are being used like this all over the world?"

Instantly, he exuded comfort. "We have laws. Human females are never allowed to be afraid."

Shaking my head, I countered, "I've been afraid."

Long-fingered hands reached toward my face, settling lightly to cup my cheek. "You're special, Emily. Resistant to suggestion. You see things the rest of your kind cannot."

That niggling thought that had twisted in my brain from the day the ships landed, I had to say it out loud. "Because this is an invasion."

"It is."

Honesty... felt right.

A nonviolent takeover of my entire species, one happening right before our eyes. "What do you want from us?"

The tips of his fingers began lightly burrowing against my scalp. "Companionship. We do not pair with one another. Adults must find a compatible species, adapt to them, and integrate. Humans are extremely compatible."

He'd failed to mention something extremely obvious. "But only the women."

Phi nodded, another of our mannerisms he'd picked up. "Males of your species cannot bear children. That makes them superfluous."

And our males now had short lifespans, lived only long enough to increase the gene pool. Leaving billions of women with no options for a partner. "You *are* the reason my brother is dying. Your people did this to us."

"Without our interference, environmental factors would have wiped out your entire species in less than one hundred Earth years. Humanity would have died out. We offered a solution, adjusted one genetic variable to maximize the female population. Making the expense and exertion of resources worth our effort."

Pulling my head away from his hands, I felt tears spill from my eyes. "As your reward?"

"I know you feel as if I have betrayed you, but I have come here to save you. Is it impossible to imagine you will be happy with me? Am I really so different from a human man?"

No. Every time I saw him, he looked, and behaved, a little more human. His skill in mimicry was astounding. And just like a human man, he was using me for sex... *or something*.

Rounding the counter, Phi reached for me, his black eyes wide and vulnerable. "Where are your thoughts, Emily?"

Hopping off the sticky stool, I backed away, my hand up in warning for him not to come closer. "Aren't you afraid I'm going to tell everyone what you've said? Aren't you afraid I'll tell them what you are?"

Canting his head to the side, he studied me—my posture, my expression—and I was certain, my mind. "What would it change? They can't hear you. They only hear what we tell them to hear. Why upset their happy existence? Why not embrace the fact that my kind offered your kind *life*?"

"At a price!" My brother's future, for example.

"Please, Emily. Would you rather your species go extinct?"

No, of course not. But I was torn; somewhat relieved he'd confirmed I wasn't crazy, really confused… I was a mess. Were Phi's kind an infection or an inoculation? "I love my brother."

"Because of your memories of the lake?" Phi dared to step closer, to pin me between the wall and his body. "Emily, you've never been to that lake. The memory you cling to is a tool, a fabricated scenario that brings you joy—we add ourselves into the moment. But, the implantation has not worked properly on you. You were never supposed to envision your brother. You were only to see me. I am the one who enjoys swimming and desires to take his life partner to the lake. The home you see in the background is mine. *I built it for us.*"

That could not be true. I remembered that day perfectly, could hear water slapping the dock. If I turned my head, my brother would be in the lake, waving at me to jump in.

But a knife of cruel words cut through the comforting memory. "Your brother only calls when your monthly check is late or if he needs more money. He gambles with it. You know that, and it makes you very sad. You have had an exceptionally lonely life."

Sudden painful gloom fell over my heart. It was hard to swallow, hard to feel anything but intense depression. Depression even the brightest shade of cheap fuchsia curtains could not relieve.

And Phi was responsible for it. He was bringing on this horror. And I struck, with all the force a pathetic human female might wield against a massive, muscular alien. "You're making me feel this way."

He never so much as flinched. Instead, he tried to pet my head. "No. I'm doing nothing. This is how you feel without my intervention. This is who you were before you met me."

I must have looked like a heartbroken child, my arms fast around my middle as if I might hug myself well. Eyes wide, a lost expression on my face, I began to cry. "Please stop."

But it only grew worse. Weighing me down to a floor too fancy for a woman of my standing to even look at.

"At first glance, I knew I wanted you. And with one brush of my mind, I believe it may have been the first time you'd smiled, really smiled, in years. The more I learned about your life, the more I had to intervene. It gives me pain to know you were sad for so long."

God, I was drowning in it—the mundane existence, the toil, the work that never got me anywhere. The calls. So many calls for more money, knowing that no matter what I gave him, it was never enough. "This can't be real!"

Phi pulled the fancy phone he'd given me out of his pocket and put it in my hands. "Call him. Talk to him. Ask your brother about the lake."

Chapter Nine

New phone in hand, I found my way out to Phi's balcony. Standing in the open air as if it might offer privacy. How ridiculous I was. Gripping that present. That extremely expensive smart device. I wanted to chuck it over the railing and watch it sail down and shatter dozens of floors below on the roadway.

Because I could still hear my brother yelling, *"What do you mean you got fired? What the fuck is wrong with you?"*

He had not been happy to hear from me at all.

Between the hacking cough and the lecture about responsibility, he'd reminded me that his kids required school supplies, clothing, a roof over their heads, and that it was my job as family to provide it. After all, he couldn't work, and his wife had to rear the children. How could she be expected to support them financially?

I felt cold, hollow, and overfull all at the same time.

I felt unloved.

"Get another goddamn job right now!"

How had my life become this? Wake up, work. Come home, sleep. Over and over with nary a day off and nothing to show for it.

Everything Phi had said was true. The awfulness I felt in that moment *was* my life, had been my life for so long I had grown accustomed to the grind. Before Phi had messed with my mind, it had felt normal. And having felt joy thanks to his machinations, I wish I had never learned differently.

The sliding door behind me opened.

He said, "That first day, you smiled at me. You recognized me. One touch of our minds and you no longer felt alone." A hand landed lightly on my shoulder. He squeezed, kneading where I was tense. "It is difficult for new worlds to know us at first, but it soon becomes natural. I promise you this."

Phi made it sound, and *feel*, like it might be so simple.

Nothing in life was simple. "You're a different species."

Gentle as a breeze, his voice fell upon me in a way I'd never heard a human man speak. "It's no different than meeting a person from a distant culture."

Closing my eyes, I took a shaking breath. I could imagine the protocol, the odds of how these aliens operated, what they must have done to prepare. Because I might have worked as a waitress, but like most people in service, I was anything but stupid. "What do you know of Earth's cultures? How many languages can you speak?"

"All of them." He moved so his arm draped over my shoulder, tucking me to his side. Where life was steady, warm. Where I was sheltered from the wind. "I was unsure in which country I would find my life partner. Find you."

And I was uneducated, with a shitty resume, and very little self-confidence at that moment. Hell, I hardly

94

spoke English well. Forget about my spelling abilities. "I need to go home."

Stroking my hair, Phi said, "You won't feel better if you go back to that place and isolate yourself."

Eyes shut tight, an ache in my head building, I had to disagree. Already a list of restaurants was forming in my thoughts, places I could apply to at once. One of them would hire me. I could probably start working in a day or two. I could get money for my brother. He'd never need to tell me I was worthless again.

Unless one of Phi's cronies snatched me off the street to try to *assimilate* me against my will like he'd said. The very thought was repugnant. I was not even sure if Phi had told me the truth. Though at this point, why lie?

The statement probably made no sense, but I said it anyway. "It was easier before I knew it could be different."

"My intentions were never to cause you despair. But, it might simplify your understanding of all I offer. Your life with me will be full, happy, and safe."

"And what about my family?"

"They have used you long enough."

That was not good enough, not by a long shot. Two children depended on me to survive. Turning my head to meet his inhuman eyes, I hardened my resolve. "I need to go home."

I could see that he was tempted to voodoo my head, the *click, click, click* ready to go. "May I walk you there? Just to the door?"

Considering I had no pants, I'd need a large male at my side should something go even more wrong.

I also really didn't want to be alone. "Okay."

* * *

I didn't need to look out the peephole to know Phi was standing guard in my hallway. I could feel him somehow. He was not deadening my melancholy, but he was somehow whispering in my mind that he was there when I was ready.

I wasn't ready.

The milk in my fridge had turned. Eating stale cereal dry, I sat on the edge of my bed and stared out the window. The neighboring building's brick façade looked the same as it always did—sloppy mortar squishing out, age-worn bricks having somehow turned moldy with time.

What a view.

How many years had I lived in this apartment?

I'd probably die in this apartment... surrounded by cheap throw pillows and dirty laundry, fast food taco grease under my fingernails.

Seriously, what the fuck was Phi thinking following me around?

That's right, to assimilate me.

I still wasn't sure what that meant beyond the suddenly radiant skin and something a bit more disturbing I'd discovered while trying to give myself a pep talk in the bathroom mirror.

Where the button-down shirt parted, where I was flushed from being upset, I'd seen a subtle pattern under my skin.

Something similar to stripes.

Not similar to… exactly like. Stripes marked the dark skin of my chest.

What had he said? Twice while we'd fucked he'd given and taken just enough?

Now, he looked more human, and I looked more alien.

Would people on the street even notice it? How far could alien mind games extend?

Were the lines going to get brighter or fade away if I never let him touch me again?

I'd stared, running my fingers over the shimmering pattern, and then I'd unbuttoned the shirt. Naked, I found they were everywhere, hard to see unless I was flustered, but there.

They were even pretty in a Halloween costume kind of way. Take me to a nightclub and I'd probably glow under the lights—to warn off other aliens that I had already been claimed.

That had to be what they were, and there were too many other things going on in my head for me to decide if I was angry about it.

I might have even been grateful. The picture he'd painted of mind-manipulated women being dragged off the street terrified me.

How long would it be before most females bore marks?

This might be the new norm. Fashionable even.

I had not been fashionable a day in my life.

My go-to was natural curls, drugstore makeup, second-hand clothes… and now stripes.

Deep down, the more I thought of it, the more I understood they'd never fade. The only thing that would shift them would be another green man's attempt at assimilation. I'd have stripes, or polka dots, or wiggly swirls—one of them would write their signature on my skin.

Because we'd been invaded and everything was going to change.

As stupid as it sounded, I couldn't decide what major issue I should focus on. There were just too damn many: Invasion, the silvery-green hopeful 'life partner' standing in my hall, the fact I needed a new job immediately, the fake memory of the lake, my brother, my shit life... I could go on.

Overwhelmed, and decidedly sorry for myself, I flopped down in bed and chose to ignore them all.

Except, I couldn't. Lying there, hugging a purple pillow with gold tassels, I could not stop thinking. I guess when you're really low, you make foolish decisions. That's how people got hooked on heroin, right? Junkies just wanted to feel better.

A tattered robe hanging from my droopy shoulders, I went to my door and undid the bolt.

Phi said nothing, patient as ever.

"No sex—or whatever you call it."
I said these words then opened the door
wider so he might come in.

And come in he did. He came in,
walked me to my bed, and lay down with
me while I fingered the tassels of my
favorite pillow and stared off into space.

It was hours of silence before I fell
asleep, his bicep under my head and his
arm around my middle.

My only words before I closed my
eyes were, "I'm not sure about the silver
stripes."

Lips came to my ear, a soft
squeeze around my waist reassuring. "I
think they're beautiful."

Chapter Ten

I'll take the blame. I started it.

No dreams of the lake had come to warm me, no mental mishmash of alien voodoo—and for some reason, waking that way, knowing Phi had not tried his tricks, was a comfort I couldn't describe.

I knew he could have done it; it would have made his objective easier. But, he'd respected my feelings, both spoken and unspoken on the subject. Which made me feel... *nice*.

Nice enough that I wasn't burdened by constant suspicion. Nice enough that when I woke up and he was still there beside me, I didn't immediately freak out.

Instead, I studied him, the alien man that never slept. I even let my fingers explore.

It didn't start off sexual. Phi didn't try to touch me back; he let every decision be mine.

Meeting his eyes felt too intimate, so instead, I studied the planes of his face, the stripes, the lips and jaw I now understood *had changed* to appear more human. I even touched them. They were warm, like mine. Appealing.

His adaptation was targeted, after all, to charm me.

Skull smooth, ears smaller and shaped slightly differently than a human, I explored these parts too. Sensitive lobes led to the man closing his eyes and drawing in a breath when I traced them. Knowing I'd inadvertently given him pleasure… excited me.

Abandoning ears for neck, I followed the line of his throat until his shirt stopped further exploration.

What would happen if I popped the first button, and then the next, and the next? What would happen if I did these things and still told him no?

Would he listen? Would he pressure me for sex like most human men would?

He answered my thoughts. "I am honored you wish to familiarize yourself with my body."

Darting my attention up to meet his eyes, I sucked my full lower lip, unsure what to say. "No mind tricks."

I swear, he smirked. "I can lie still. You may do what you wish."

Sitting up on a hip, I did exactly that. I undid his shirt, spread the fabric, and stared down at a powerful chest: smooth, striped, and lean. Right down the middle was the line I liked best, the one that bisected his face, his neck, his body, as if perfectly segmenting him in two. Tracing it, I followed the bumps of musculature, on a body with no belly button, wondering if these were a sign of whatever species had mothered him.

How had he been born? What planet had his forbearer found a 'life partner' on?

Maybe he'd been hatched?

The only things I knew about Phi were that he loved to eat pie, had a penchant for swimming, and that he'd built me a house by a lake. He had also shown himself to be a giving lover.

And had tentacles around his wang...

"Where are you from?"

"A world with lots of water. My mother, for lack of a better word, was amphibious."

So yes, he'd been hatched. And also, yes, he was poking around in my thoughts.

"I will respect your desire that I not implant any suggestions, but it's impossible for me to not have a general idea of what you are thinking."

And it was aggravating. "Why go to the trouble of speaking then?"

"Because you cannot know me any other way. I want you to know me. I want you to know I'm an architect, that I enjoy your earth, that I can't see color like you can."

Arching a brow, I teased, "You can't see color?"

"Only grayscale. When you think of me as silvery-green, I do not know what that means."

At least there was some way I had the upper hand. Smug, I leered and went right back to exploring.

His hand came up, catching a stray curl to tuck behind my ear. "It amuses you?"

It did. There was a whole mess of colorblind aliens walking over my planet who'd never understand a great deal of human opinion on art, fashion, flowers...

That made those things mine.

Stopping at his waistband, I found I did have a question I wanted a direct answer to. "How much more is your body going to change?"

"It depends on what is needed to make us fully compatible." Phi offered me the subtle reminder that I too was changing, augmenting his answer when I grew nervous. "The majority of adaptation will take place on my end."

Which begged the greater question...

106

My smirk vanished, and I sat back, pulling my hand from his body. "What does it mean to be assimilated? If one of you are going to do it to me, I have a right to know."

A new expression crossed Phi's face, the expression of possessiveness. "I won't let another of my kind assimilate you. I will be the one to take you as life partner."

It didn't seem I had much say in it. "You said you'd removed other challengers?"

Sitting up, so much taller than I, he looked down at me and grew a bit fierce. "Removed. Yes."

Creepy. I was pretty sure removed meant murdered... and a flicker of imagination and the following mental imagery showed a differing version of Phi lurking behind me, sometimes splattered in slivery green fluid. A constant shadow always waiting... and then a more comforting idea took its place... he'd kept me safe.

I walked home from work nightly, sometimes I'd heard things. More than once I had been touched.

But was that a lake memory or a real memory, and with so much comfort close by, why should I care?

"We have developed a proclivity for human pleasure. There are not many species that reproduce in such an exquisite fashion." He shifted again, moving forward so I had no choice but to move back. In three seconds, he had me pressed against my pillows, hovering with a hungry grin on his face. "As such, fifteen already have attempted to have a taste of you. More will try, unless…"

I knew what he was getting at. "…I let you do what you want to me."

He stretched like a lazy beast drinking in the sun, settling even more firmly atop my body. "I could make love to you every hour of every day, over and over until there was nothing left of either of us."

Even if I wasn't looking for physical release in that moment, his words did stir a grand twinge down below. "You didn't answer my question."

"It is different with every pairing. In your transition, your dark skin has begun to mimic my dermal patterns, your metabolism has increased, your immune system is fortified, and I expect you will live decades longer than your un-partnered contemporaries.

Even more spilled from his definitely fuller lips, "Your reproductive system will alter slightly to accommodate our future children, and your skill at evading my suggestions will most likely expand." Those black eyes looked about ready to eat me. "Nothing can be sure until transition is complete. But I can say, you will be even more perfect than you already are."

Cornered, I felt I had very little say in my future. Not that I'd had really any say in my life up until this point. "What about what I want?"

It seemed as if my question was exactly the one he'd been waiting for me to ask. "Tell me what you want. Give me the opportunity to prove I can make you happy."

No one had ever asked me that before.

Yes, I'd led the conversation this direction, but hearing him ask me directly, I had no idea what to say.

I had no idea what I wanted. Mentally stumbling in search of an answer, all I could blurt out was, "I need to find a new job."

"But what do you *want*, Emily?"

Once, a long time ago, I'd wanted to go to college. Saying it out loud seemed wrong though. College was for people who had a future beyond supporting others.

He might not have been playing his tricks, but he was still in my head. Looking to comfort me, Phi maneuvered so he could cup my cheek as he said, "There is nothing wrong in seeking to expand your knowledge. A mind like yours is wasted as a waitress."

It might have been the nicest thing anyone had ever said to me. It didn't change facts. "I can't afford it."

"Your brother does not own you anymore." An unspoken *I do* was impossible to miss. Just as impossible to miss as his forming sex organ poking me below. "My life partner will go to college if she wishes."

It seemed as if the offer was on the table. I'd spread my legs and let him inside my body, and in turn he would offer my dreams on a silver platter. "What about his children?"

"If you let me kiss you, Emily, I give you my word the monthly check will be sent." His lips hovering over mine, he whispered, "But he will never be allowed to speak to you again the way he did today. Human males have grown repugnant in their decline."

On that, we were agreed.

The fairytale... the silliness of the situation... I grasped it. Who talked like this? Who actually was tempted to be swept away by a practical stranger—a green Prince Charming?

I was.

The idea of spending one more day in my sad apartment made me want to scream. And so I sold my soul to a creature that might have been the devil for all I knew. "Where do you want to kiss me?"

Phi didn't hesitate to reach between my legs and grab where I ached. "Here."

I let him. I let him do anything he wished, powerless to say no when each nerve was singing, and pleasure eclipsed my endless worries. Coming more times than I could count, I even looked forward to the *pop* of his impending release and to the pain that would follow.

And follow it did. Phi was determined in his attempt to complete assimilation. Lying under him, twisted by barbs that dug through organs and flesh, I screamed as I paid the price he exacted.

When it was over, I was in shock, shaking, cold, and unable to complain when he wrapped me in a blanket and carried me through the streets all the way back to his apartment.

112

Chapter Eleven

I don't recall how many days, how many months it took. The change wasn't… describable. Tucked back in his city apartment, I was fucked day and night, fed sweet things, given water. In a daze, more of me altered and less of me remained the same. I think a winter might have come and gone, but my hazy recollection would never play fair if I put forth the massive effort required to consider it.

I suppose that was what a mind did to protect itself from the body's trauma.

He came in me, and came in me, and came in me until that *pop* was synonymous with release. My release from too much pleasure. My release from whatever I had been before.

Undulating like a massive tongue one moment, wriggling and throbbing and going so far as to rattle, his organ worked me beyond frenzy, his beautiful mouth tracing my glimmering stripes. Tongue licking at them.

As I grew stronger, he grew rougher. Sexual play by his kind nothing like bland human fucking.

Sometimes he scared me in the most intense moments. In the moments where I knew he wanted his barbs to dig deeper, to alter more, to make me spun out and breedable.

I told him I was not ready for children. Panted it into his shoulder when I felt something new come from his cock.

And as he always did, Phi listened. Slowed his assault, still stroking my clit with those feelers, and swore to me no such decision would be made until we both were in agreement it was time to mate to such a degree.

A part of me felt it was wrong for softening toward him even more at such a statement.

"I love you, Emily. Your joy is my joy."

Yet something still was steadily pumping inside my body. I didn't know what it was, for it sealed itself inside my womb, bulging out my belly for days. It must have been absorbed within me, for no gush broke free later to drip down my thighs when my monthly cycle arrived.

He found menstruation fascinating, eager to provide whatever I required to be comfortable.

It did not stop him from fucking me. It did not stop me from orgasming even harder than I ever had before.

And then one day I woke up, saw the rising sun out the window and realized I was no longer in the city. The room was familiar; I had been in it for weeks. Right?

It smelled of Phi, of me, of a great deal of sex.

And it was our room in the cabin he had built for me.

Life continued. I noticed more.

I noticed that joy had the flavors of strawberries and fine coffee.

Spoiled rotten, that's what I was.

I wasn't keen on all of it, but what relationship was flawless?

Phi had become more human, his eyes had even adapted just enough that he could see my world in color. And it had thrilled him. I'll never forget the way he looked at me that first day, how he had spent ages describing in all the ways my black skin was more glorious than any bloom in his garden. That my soft, springy hair was tactilely glorious, tangling his long fingers in my natural curls to enjoy the texture and *play*. My hair, he confessed, had been the first thing about me that had caught his eye. The second was my rump.

Yes, he used the word rump. And I forgave him for it when he took great handfuls of my generous ass and practically purred.

Being like me in any way had thrilled him. His laughter and smiles more addictive than any drug.

My stripes brightened to an extreme, true silver on rich brown skin, but no human seemed to notice. Phi's alien buddies certainly did. Their eyes followed me when I walked around the nearby town as if I were some mythical creature they'd heard stories about but had never seen in person.

Self-conscious, I kept mostly covered unless at home, where I kept mostly naked.

And yes, my home had changed. I understood that now. There had not been room in my old apartment to study, no table to spread out worksheets or pile up books. Phi had a desk just for my use in our beautiful home, a pretty lamp, supplies, all beside French doors with an actual view... of water.

Just like he had a bedroom for me, fresh food in the fridge, and new clothing waiting should I want to wear it.

University was a year or two away, but my catch-up courses at a nearby community college were going well. Surprisingly, I wasn't the oldest or the only *striped* student in the class. There were three other women just like me. Their markings were different and their life partners were strangers, but we each had a similar story.

We each had the chance at a real future now.

We each went home to someone who was loving, giving, sweet, and attentive.

I made friends.

I also worked part-time as a waitress, because I wanted to. My tables were predominantly seated by males of the alien variety who wished to converse with me as if I might disclose a great secret. Their eyes often lingered on the sometimes obvious bulge in my belly should I have been fucked before my shift. The *things* that Phi put in me that never came out.

I grew not to mind, though I never once let one of them touch. On occasion, the more daring of our new invaders would ask. Some even looked unbearably heartbroken.

I dared not think of why. Perhaps loneliness? Had they not found success in the females they pursued?

Had they tried and the barbs did more damage than was reparable? Should I worry over such things?

Phi assured me repeatedly that lowly labor was unnecessary, that interaction with any of his species I did not enjoy was preventable… that he could provide everything I needed.

But I needed to work, to feel independent. I even enjoyed it more knowing I was working for myself and no one else. It was my money, I spent it anyway I wished… almost always on presents for my brother's kids who I actually had time to visit now.

Said brother? Phi never left me alone with him. Not once in all the months since I'd awoken in his house by the lake. I knew why. Phi was making him be gracious. Phi was *suggesting* the man spend the money provided by us on his children and his children alone.

Whether the suggestions stuck after we left, I didn't know. All I knew was that once I got over my pride, I'd never been more grateful to anyone in my life. Phi had kept his word, taken my burden from me and shouldered it himself.

He wasn't lacking for money. Somehow these aliens had a better grasp of our economy than we did. They controlled everything.

Only it didn't look that way unless you squinted just right.

I'd stopped looking. If these creatures had come here to make other women as happy as I'd become, then they were welcome with open arms.

I *was* happy.

I felt like I mattered.

Phi loved me.

I was growing to love him in a way I never knew I might feel.

The breeze shifted, bringing the salty tang of the lake to tickle my nose. I heard a splash and my name on the wind. There was someone waving from the water—someone silvery-green and very beautiful, beckoning me to leave my studies and run outside to play.

I knew exactly *what kind of play* Phi liked to enjoy in the water, and I bit my lower lip, grinning stupidly as I stood up to join him.

Thank you for reading STRANGEWAYS! Keep an eye out for more tales of these invaders and the ladies they claim!

Sign up for my newsletter 🐾
http://bit.ly/AddisonCainNewsletter

Craving more? Omegaverse Dark Romance at its most gut-wrenching! Jealous, possessive, and willing to commit any sin to steal his mate, Shepherd is the antihero book boyfriend you've been waiting for.

- **Born to be Bound** — Violent, calculating, and incapable of remorse, Shepherd demands his new mate's adoration. Her attention. Her body.
- **Born to be Broken** — He doesn't know how to love his captive Omega. But Shepherd is determined to learn.

- **Reborn** — the nature of their pair-bond has consumed Claire to the point that she has difficulty differentiating where her feelings begin and Shepherd's machinations end.
- **Stolen** —He took her with violence while none intervened. He broke her, swearing he'd put her back together.

The Wren's Song Series is a dark, sinister Omegaverse Reverse Harem tale for those with twisted tastes and a love for complete power exchange.

- **Branded Captive** — Wren can't sing like a bird. She can't speak at all. The Alpha kingpin and his pack didn't buy the Omega to hear it talk.

- **Silent Captive** — Wren is caught in the clutches of three dangerous Alphas, each with their own selfish designs.
- **Broken Captive** — Caspian has marked her, Toby has claimed her, and Kieran is unwillingly caught in her spell.
- **Ravaged Captive** — Drenched in wealth and power, Caspian holds my city by the throat. No man or woman denies him, not even me.

Carnal, filthy, and unbelievably satisfying. My bestselling Omegaverse Dark Romance awaits those daring enough to take a taste.

- **The Golden Line** — They call me brutal. They call me unrepentant. They call me possessive. I am all these things and much, *much* worse.

Like your men in doting, affectionate, and utterly possessive? Read my Reverse Harem Dark Romance. The Irdesi Empire Series is smoldering page-turner sure to satisfy.

- **Sigil** — He will have her. Even if he must crush empires. Even if he must harm her for her own good. Even if he must share her with his brothers. Sigil will be his.
- **Sovereign** — Sovereign tends his reluctant consort. His many Brothers lavish her with attention, each exercising their own brand of seduction to woo their species' only female.

If your tastes run to brooding alpha males, my hit dark romance, this Regency Dark Romance will scratch your itch.

- **Dark Side of the Sun** — Greedy, cunning, cruel, Gregory claims to love her, offers to kill for her… but lies come easily to his tongue.

Obsession and the most twisted "love" fill this smoldering page-turner. Beware, these vampires don't play nice.

- **Catacombs** — The vampire king has found his queen, locking her away for his own sick pleasures.
- **Cathedral** — Malcom defies the king of evil himself to possess

the one woman he knows must be his.

Taboo horror that will worm its way into your darker thoughts and keep you up all night? Whatever you do, don't follow the white rabbit!

- **The White Queen** — The devil owes the Hatter a favor… and he knows just what he wants for his prize.
- **Immaculate** — But my knees have been sullied in worship to a vacant altar. Everything I was taught is a lie. There is no God here.

Love good, old fashioned desire? Take a turn with this prohibition era romance.

- **A Taste of Shine** —
Something isn't right about the new girl in town. Charlotte Elliot swears, she drinks, and she's trying too damn hard to fit in with the simple folk.

- **A Shot in the Dark** —
Matthew is determined to find his run-away sweetheart. And then he's going to marry her.

Join my Facebook group, Addison Cain's Dark Longing's Lounge, for sneak peeks, free loot, and a whole lot of fun! Ask me anything! I'd love to chat with you.

Now, please enjoy an excerpt of BORN TO BE BOUND!

BORN TO BE BOUND

She watched him bolt the door with a rod so thick it dwarfed her ankle, trapping her, cornering the Omega for mating. Unsure if Shepherd had heard, she used her feet to scoot away from the male until her back hit the wall, and tried again. "Food… we can't go out... hunted, forced. They're killing us." Her blown pupils looked up at the intimidating male and pleaded for him to understand. "You are *the* Alpha in Thólos, you hold control... we have no one else to ask."

"So you foolishly walked into a room full of feral males to ask for food?" He was mocking her, his eyes mean, even as he grinned.

The horror of the day, the sexual frustration of her heat, made Claire belligerently raise her head and meet his eyes. "If we don't get food, I'm dead anyway."

Seeing the female grimace through another cramping wave, Shepherd growled, an instinctual reaction to a breeding Omega. The noise shot right between her legs, full of the promise of everything she needed. His second, louder grumbled noise sang inside her, and a wave of warm slick drenched the floor below her swollen sex, saturating the air to entice him.

She could not take it. "Please don't make that noise."

"You are fighting your cycle," he grunted low and abrasive, beginning to pace, watching her all the while.

Shaking her head back and forth, Claire began to murmur, "I've lived a life of celibacy."

Celibacy? That was unheard of... a rumored story. Omegas could not fight the urge to mate. That was why the Alphas fought for them and forced a pair-bond to keep them for themselves. The smell alone drove any Alpha into a rut.

He growled again and the muscles of her sex clenched so hard she whined and curled up on the floor.

It was hard enough to make it through estrous locked in a room alone until the cycle broke, but his damn noise and the smell invading past the rotting stickiness of her clothing was breaking her insides apart.

The degrading way he spoke made her open her eyes to see the beast standing still, his massive erection apparent despite layers of clothing. "How long does your heat typically last, Omega?"

Shivering, suddenly loving the sound of that lyrical rasp, she clenched her fists at her sides instead of beckoning him nearer. "Four days, sometimes a week."

"And you have been through them all in seclusion instead of submitting to an Alpha to break them?"

"Yes."

He was making her angry, furious even, with his stupid questions. Every part of her was screaming out that he should be stroking her and easing the need. *That it was his job!* With her hand still pressed over her nose and mouth, her muffled, broken explanation came as a jumbled, angry rant, Claire hissing, "I choose."

He just laughed, a cruel, coarse sound.

Omegas had become exceptionally rare since the plagues and the following Reformation Wars a century prior. That made them a valuable commodity which

Alphas in power took as if it was their due. And in a city brimming with aggressive Alphas like Thólos, she'd been trapped in a life of feigning existence as a Beta just to live unmolested, spent a small fortune on heat-suppressants, and locked herself away with the other few celibates she knew when estrous came. Hidden in plain sight before Shepherd's army sprung out of the Undercroft and the government was slaughtered, their corpses left strung up from the Citadel like trophies.

Claire had been forced into hiding the very next day, when the unrest inspired the lower echelons of population to challenge for dominance. Where there had been order, suddenly all Thólos knew was anarchy. Those awful men just took any Omega they could find; killing mates and children in order to keep the women—to breed them or fuck until they died.

"What is your name?"

She opened her eyes, elated he was listening. "Claire."

"How many of you are there, little one?"

Trying to focus on a spot on the wall instead of the large male and where his beautiful engorged dick was challenging the zipper of his trousers, she turned her head to where her body craved to nest, staring with hunger at the collection of colorful blankets, pillows—a bed where everything must be saturated by his scent.

An extended growl warned, "You are losing your impressive focus, little one. How many?"

Her voice broke. "Less than a hundred... We lose more every day."

"You have not eaten. You're hungry." It was not a question, but spoken with such a low vibration that his hunger for *her* was apparent.

"Yesss." It was almost a whine. She was so near to pleading, and it wasn't going to be for food.

The prolonged answering growl of the beast compelled a gush of slick to wet her so badly, she was left sitting in a slippery puddle. Doubling over, frustrated and needy, she sobbed, "Please don't make that noise," and immediately the growl changed pitch. Shepherd began to purr for her.

There was something so infinitely soothing in that low rumble that she sighed audibly and did not bolt at his slow, measured approach. She watched him with such attention, her huge, dilated pupils a clear mark that she was so very close to falling completely into estrous.

Even when Shepherd crouched down low, he towered over her, all bulging muscle and musky sweat. She tried to say the words, *"Only instincts..."* but jumbled them so badly their meaning was lost.

Starting with the scarf, he unwound the items that tainted her beautiful pheromones, purring and stroking every time she whimpered or shifted nervously. When he pulled her forward to take away the reeking cloak, her eyes drew level with his confined erection. Claire's uncovered nose sniffed automatically at the place where his trousers bulged. In that moment all she wanted, all that she had ever wanted, was to be fucked, knotted, and bred by that male.

Only instincts...

Shepherd pressed his face to her neck and sucked in a long breath, groaning as his cock jumped and began to leak to please her. He had gone into the rut, there was no changing that fact, and with it came a powerful need to see the female filled with seed, to soothe what was driving her to rub against her hand in such a frenzy.

The words were almost lost in her breath, "You need to lock me in a room for a few days..."

A feral grin spread. "You are locked in a room, little one, with the Alpha who killed ten men and two of his sworn Followers to bring you here." He stroked her hair, petting her because something inside told him his hands could calm her. "It's too late now. Your defiant celibacy is over. Either you submit willingly to me where I will rut you through your heat, or you may leave out that door where my men will, no doubt, mount you in the halls once they smell you."

Ready for more?
Read Born to be Bound now!

Addison Cain

USA TODAY bestselling author and Amazon Top 25 bestselling author, Addison Cain is best known for her dark romances, smoldering Omegaverse, and twisted alien worlds. Her antiheroes are not always redeemable, her lead females stand fierce, and nothing is ever as it seems.

Deep and sometimes heart wrenching, her books are not for the faint of heart. But they are just right for those who enjoy unapologetic bad boys, aggressive alphas, and a hint of violence in a kiss.

Visit her website: addisoncain.com

Sign up for her newsletter:
http://bit.ly/AddisonCainNewsletter

Don't miss these exciting titles by Addison Cain!

Omegaverse:
The Golden Line

The Alpha's Claim Series:
Born to be Bound
Born To Be Broken
Reborn
Stolen
Corrupted (coming soon)

Wren's Song Series:
Branded Captive
Silent Captive
Broken Captive
Ravaged Captive

The Irdesi Empire Series:
Sigil
Sovereign
Que (coming soon)

Cradle of Darkness
Catacombs
Cathedral
The Relic

A Trick of the Light Duet:

A Taste of Shine
A Shot in the Dark

Historical Romance:
Dark Side of the Sun

Horror:
The White Queen
Immaculate

CPSIA information can be obtained
at www.ICGtesting.com
Printed in the USA
LVHW032119201021
701017LV00001B/1